Catch of tl

written by Dawn McMillan
illustrated by Enrique Vignolo

Luke felt excited as the boat slid off the trailer into the water.
Today was going to be a great day for fishing, and he was glad
that his friend Alex had come along too. He liked his company,
and he liked the delicious pizza that Alex always brought on
their fishing trips.

2

The sea was calm as they headed out across the bay. Sea birds flew ahead of them, expecting fish, and Luke thought that was a good sign. At the deepest part of the bay, Luke's Dad shut off the motor. With the anchor down and the boat settled, they all baited their hooks and let their lines down into the water. They waited, and they waited. They changed their baits, and they waited.

4

"I can't believe it! We've been here for ages without even a bite!"
Luke complained. "Perhaps we should have our lunch early, in
case the fish start biting later."

"Luke," his Dad laughed, "you're always hungry, but I reckon
we should move closer to shore. See, the water's starting to get
choppy. Conditions can change quite quickly in this bay. Let's stay
safe and head in."

Luke felt glad that they were heading in. Dad was right.
The wind had swung around, and the waves were getting bigger.
He sat quietly holding onto the side as the boat bounced beneath
him, and he wasn't so sure he wanted lunch after all.

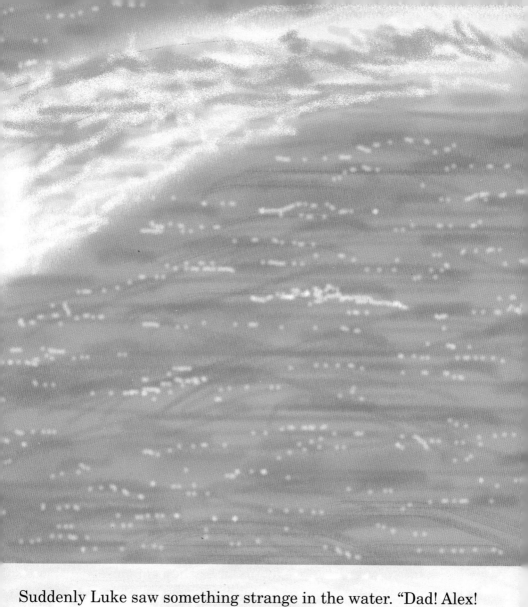

Suddenly Luke saw something strange in the water. "Dad! Alex!
Look over there!" he shouted. "What's that?"

"Where?" Dad asked, squinting his eyes against the glittering sea.
"Well, it might be a buoy from a net," he suggested, "but we'll check
it out. Hang on tight – I'll circle around to have a better look."

"It looks like a boat," Luke exclaimed as they got closer.
"It's a kayak, I think, and it's upside down!"
He sat at the rear of the boat, his face white, the noise of
the boat motor drowning out his whisper, "What if...?"
Then he yelled, "There's someone there! A person wearing
a lifejacket!"

"Quick, let's get over there!" Dad shouted. "Luke, grab my cell phone. Call the emergency number and explain what's happening. Say we're straight out from Jackson's Bay, just east of the lighthouse."

He slowed down, moving the boat closer to the overturned craft. "Hang on there!" he yelled. "Hang on!"

14

As Luke made the call, Alex leaned out from the side of the boat. He could see that the shape in the water was a kayak, with a young woman holding on to it with one hand. "Hang on! We're coming!" he called to her. But at that moment the woman lost her grip and the kayak drifted away.

"Grab the rope, boys!" shouted Dad. "Quick! Give it to me. Take the wheel, Luke. Hold the boat steady! Give it just a little bit of speed. Good work. We're getting closer!" he said, as he threw the rope toward the woman.

"Grab the rope! Grab the rope!" Luke yelled, his heart racing in fear "Please," breathed Alex, feeling despair when she reached weakly and failed to grasp it.

"This time!" yelled Dad, throwing the rope again. "Yes!" he shouted in relief, as the rope splashed down right in front of the floundering woman, and she took hold of it with both hands. "Hang on!" the boys called together as Dad pulled the rope toward the boat. "Kick!" added Luke. "You're nearly there!" "Up you come!" said Dad as he helped the woman up the ladder. "You're safe now. Bring our thermal blanket, Luke," he said. "It's in the First Aid Kit."

The woman shook as Luke wrapped the blanket around her. "I'm so lucky you came," she whispered, trembling as tears rolled down her face. "I drifted too far out, and then the kayak capsized when those giant waves came up. I thought it was all over for me." Luke thought he might cry, too. "It's okay now," he said gently. "Alex's got you a hot drink from our flask. Would you like a slice of pizza? You must be starving after that ordeal!"

"Sounds good, but later, okay?" the woman smiled weakly. "Thank you. Thank you all. You're amazing."

"Well, we went fishing today and didn't catch a single fish," Luke told her, "but we're really glad we caught you!"